ANGUS MACGREGOR

RISE FROM *Abyss*

FALLEN ANGEL'S MISSION

THE PARDONED SERIES, BOOK 1

Hot Romance Erotica

WARNING

This book contains sexually explicit scenes and adult language. It may be considered offensive to some readers. This book is for sale to adults ONLY.

* * * * * * * * * * * * * * * * * * *

Please store your files wisely where they cannot be accessed by underage readers.

Please feel free to send me an email. Just know that these emails are filtered by my publisher. Good news is always welcome.

Angus Macgregor - **angus_macgregor@awesomeauthors.org**

You might also want to check my blog for Updates and interesting info. http://angus-macgregor.awesomeauthors.org

About the Publisher

4Fun Publishing, a member of **BLVNP Incorporated**, 340 S. Lemon #6200, Walnut CA 91789, info@blvnp.com / legal@blvnp.com
NOTE: Due to the highly emotional reaction of some people to works of erotic fiction, any email sent to the above address that contains foul language or religious references is automatically deleted by our anti-spam software and will not be seen. All other communications are welcome.

DISCLAIMER
Please don't be stupid and kill yourself. This book is a work of FICTION. Do not try any new sexual practice that you find in this book. It is fiction and not to be confused with reality. Neither the author nor the publisher or its associates assume any responsibility for any loss, injury, death or legal consequences resulting from acting on the contents in this book. Every character in this book is over 18 years of age. The author's opinions are not to be construed as the opinions of the publisher. The material in this book is for entertainment purposes ONLY. Enjoy.

The Pardoned Series, Book1

RISE FROM ABYSS

Fallen Angel's Mission

Hot Romance Erotica

By: Angus Macgregor

THE TALL man shifted his weight to his right foot and stuck out his thumb. The wind ripped through his almost shoulder length black hair as well as the long worn-out overcoat he wore, sending the fabric behind him like dark wings. He wore sunglasses but the light wasn't bright. His long black coat swirled around his tall frame like a bullfighter's cape. Nathaniel stood on the side of Hwy 11 and peered up into the Brooks Range, shrouded in mist. The air was clear blue for now, but another storm was heading this way. He had walked for so long, part in this world, part in between. Sometimes he wanted to spend all his days in the in-between. It was empty, lonely, and suited his personality.

As he stood on the empty road, the ages ran through his mind. To a mortal mind, it would be inconceivable. To him, it was just a smattering of days. He had watched the Fall of Rome and the rise of the Renaissance. Normally from afar, through the long dark void that separated this world from his prison. Even from that distant vantage point, he watched mankind grow and change, rise and fall, ascend to the heavens and probe the depths of the oceans.

His mistake had always been one of love, or at least, loving the wrong one. The Prince of Light had promised him eternal love, eternal joy, and a chance to rule the world along his side. It just made so much sense when he said it. He never stopped loving the Creator of course, he was just blinded by the light and beauty and a chance to be even closer to the other object of his love: mankind, especially the female variety.

When the rebellion began, Nathaniel's heart was broken. He never signed on for that. His mentor had promised the Creator was in agreement. His wrath had been so vast. When the forces of the Creator broke through the fortress, it was as if Nathaniel had watched his heart being ripped away from him. Then the horrible moment when the legion was cast out, like his very soul had been pierced. As the dawn of his separation from the Creator opened, Nathaniel cried out in pain and loss, to be severed from that heavenly love was beyond cost, beyond bearing.

And yet, he had endured. When most of the legion transmogrified into Lucifer's host, Nathaniel and a handful other others kept true. If there was any way to return to the Creator, he would do so. He had spent eons now in that vast blank place, neither alive nor dead, but watching...watching.

When the radiance of Michael had penetrated the void that was his home, Nathaniel could not look upon him. So long it had been since he had used his eyes to gaze upon the divine. His own angelic traits had all but disappeared over the ages. With one touch of Michael's hand, his heart surged to life. That long-dead ember flared to life and nourished his emaciated soul. When Michael spoke, it was as if thunder and lightning flashed within him.

"Would you be restored to the Creator?" the voice like hundreds of waters said.

"Yes, my brother," Nathaniel.

"It is long since you were that," Michael intoned. "But you have kept your gaze on mankind and your love for them has not diminished. If you are willing, there is a way for you to once again ascend to the heavens."

"But say the word, brother, and I will obey," Nathaniel said still with his gaze down at the ground.

Michael's fiery hand touched his face and lifted his chin. The brilliance of his person burned away so much vile corruption. He felt unencumbered from chains of his own forging for the first time in centuries. The rainbow blade that hung at his waist was pulled forth and its tip was placed on Nathaniel's chest. Michael slid the blade within, a pain like no other shuddered through him. Then a balm, sweet and languid flowed through his being and shook him to the core. When the blade was withdrawn, his shrunken, husk of a heart beat in vibrant gallops in his chest.

With that, Michael slid his hand inside the riven chest and soon thrust his entire form within Nathaniel's. The Fallen shook and trembled, vibrating with power and love. The connection was brief, but it brought him back to life. He felt a love and passion grow within his belly and groin. His member swelled to life as Michael stirred within him and soon, a cascade of urgency erupted from him in a mighty flow.

As Nathaniel opened his ice-blue eyes, Michael stood before him again.

"You will be returned to the earth. You will spend a season helping those who have never felt love, those who have given up on the idea they can be loved, and bring them back to life. You will open their hearts and bodies to all the joy and delight that the Creator intended. You will lead them toward others who will fill the empty place in their life and be the spark of love they longed for. You will trust your heart and the Creator to lead you to them, to bring them into your life. As you change them, set the glow of love ablaze within their heart, you move one step closer to your hope to be reunited. Every time you complete this one part of your journey, a new star will blaze on your arm. Today as you begin, I bequeath you the first."

Nathaniel gasped as his arm seared. He looked on his right arm where a bright blue star glimmered on his bicep. As he looked up, Michael was gone. The dark void of his captivity began to shimmer and melt away and he found himself in the bright light of an arctic morning. His nakedness was replaced with warm, soft clothes that clung to his strong frame that felt heavy and clumsy for the first time. The air was bitterly cold, yet he still felt the warmth of Michael's presence. Curious, he thought, that the Creator had started his journey here at the top of the earth. He looked either way as far as he could see and there was only whiteness that stretched on the Dalton Road in front of him. He looked up at the sky and felt the pull of the earth and knew which way was South. He walked for a time and then felt an urge he never had before. He knew what it was from all his time spent watching mankind. His bladder was close to bursting. He unfastened his pants and pulled out his member. The cool air surrounded his flesh and the heavy sack below.

He sighed and emptied his bladder into the snow, turning the white to pale yellow. The sensation was powerful and relaxed his muscles. As he held himself, he looked up and sent a prayer of thanks to the Creator. The generosity of his body was apparent and he relished the weight and strength of his penis as he finished urinating. He stood in the highway momentarily with his pants lowered, feeling the air on his flesh, feeling his manhood rise and swell as he had seen happen to mankind so often. The feeling was mesmerizing and he stroked his cock to life until it stood hard and stiff up against his belly. He knew a few more moments of this pleasuring would bring release, but he stopped and fastened up his pants. So much time to enjoy so many things, he thought.

Nathaniel heard a roar and stepped back from the road as a large truck rumbled to a stop beside him. The driver leaned over and opened the passenger door and yelled, "Are you fucking crazy? You will freeze your balls off out there. You need a ride, buddy?"

"Yes, that would be very helpful," Nathaniel said.

As the truck lumbered down the North Slope Haul Road, Nathaniel watched the bleak landscape become more forested and turn a rich verdant green. Large meandering rivers wound their way across the flat terrain like a giant braid.

"So where you headed, buddy?" the trucker asked, giving Nathaniel the once over. The trucker was a big burly young man, solid muscle, close cropped red-brown hair. Green eyes that twinkled in the bright white light.

"South," was all Nathaniel offered.

"Well, that's good. Just about every place you can go up here is south. I'm headed as far as Delta Junction."

"That sounds fine. I appreciate the ride," Nathaniel said.

The men road on in silence for some time. The trucker kept cutting his eyes over toward Nathaniel, trying to see if he could make eye contact. But Nathaniel was mesmerized by the landscape and the desolate road and endless sea of trees outside. After an hour like this, Nathaniel could feel the tension exuding from the trucker and he turned to the man to find him looking right at him.

"You're a pretty big fella, aren't you?" the trucker said.

"I suppose. You are pretty big yourself."

"Yeah, maybe so. I just have to tell you. You don't want to try any funny business with me."

"What kind of business would that be?"

"Just don't try to think you could rob me or hit on me or anything."

"I have no reason to strike you at all," Nathaniel said blank-faced.

"You're kind of weird, huh?"

Nathaniel smiled. He reached over and gripped the man's hand. The trucker's eyes flew open, but he didn't resist. Nathaniel's mind reached inside his and he saw the man's life in a flash of images that rocketed past his inner vision. "Tell me about your life, Rich," Nathaniel said.

Rich continued holding Nathaniel's hand as he drove. The man's face contorted through an array of emotions from joy to sadness, bliss to horror until finally, Nathaniel released it and touched him on the shoulder. "Tell me what is going on in your life, Rich."

With that, Rich opened up and began to spill his soul to the stranger. Born to a family in Sitka with an absent father. He had an older sister and two younger brothers. He spent his growing up years in a small single-wide trailer, sharing a room and a bed with his brothers.

"I never invited a friend over to my house, 'cause I never wanted them to see how we lived. I was so embarrassed that I had to share a bed with two boys even when I was practically a grown up. Me and my brothers actually got along good, considering we never had a moment's privacy or anything."

Rich went on to talk about leaving home as soon as he could and signing on with a crabbing boat. The work was hard and dangerous, but he did well and made good money. By the time he was twenty, he was determined to find a girl and get married.

"Don't know why I'm telling you this. I was a virgin then. Hell, I hardly jacked off all that much when I was at home because my brothers were always waking up and watching. And the other times, they were waking me up spanking it. It was just too small for us. Then the fishing boat was all men and no privacy there at all. My bunk mate would pull his cock out and stroke it almost every night. He even suggested we rub one off together. I tried it a few times and it was fine, but it just wasn't what I wanted."

Nathaniel was mesmerized by the man's story and his sad heart. In the moments they were connected, he felt the isolation and regret and defeat the man lived with and it broke his heart. Rich continued as the day grew to evening.

"After that season ended, I had a pocket full of money. I took off for Fairbanks to see what was next for me. I ended up at the University of Alaska Fairbanks, deciding to try and take a couple of classes and see if I wanted to be a student. In my first class, American history, I sat behind this girl with an auburn pony tail and a soft sweater that slipped off her shoulder so you could see her shoulder a bit. The back of her neck was smooth, the curls of hairs teasing around her ears, blowing in the wind from the open window. Her hands were small, her legs were shapely even in the tight jeans she wore."

"She sounds very nice."

"Oh brother, she was way more than nice.

"What was her name?"

"Ruby."

Rich began to share about his casual meetings with Ruby in class that turned into a date a month later. Her bright blue eyes sparkled when she smiled, which seemed like all the time. She was funny and bright, for some reason she seemed to look past all of Rich's country hick ways and see the gentle soul that resided far within. Rich felt like a million bucks with Ruby beside him in the truck or in the booth at a restaurant. She was the other half of himself he had been looking for. On their third date, laying on the couch in Rich's shabby apartment, she had grabbed his hand and slid it underneath her sweater to feel her firm breasts and nipples that rose to his touch. By the end of the date, she had pulled her sweater off and Rich had sucked the soft flesh into his mouth and swirled his tongue around the pink mounds as Ruby's head stretched back, her moans and satisfied sighs filled Rich with pleasure. He ended up blowing his wad in his shorts twice while he sucked her tits. He didn't try to go further than she seemed to want.

"I know you need more from me. Soon, I promise," she said. "I'm almost ready for you to take me. You are so sweet to wait. I will make it worth it," she said.

Rich took it to heart. He spent the next week thinking of nothing but the weekend when they would have time away from their schooling and jobs to spend two days together. Lying in bed in the evenings, Rich would stroke his cock, edging it over and over until it was throbbing, begging for release. When he finally gave in and allowed his orgasm to flow, his sperm would shoot far up on his chest or face as he thought of Ruby's hand or lips closing around him.

That weekend, the sweater came off much sooner along with her jeans and socks. She lay beside him and moved his fingers from her heaving breasts down to the damp triangle of dark red between her legs. She showed him how to stroke her clit softly and deftly until she climaxed in throbbing waves against his hand. She had him stand in front of her and she slid his jeans and underwear down, marveling at his erection. Her light touch caused Rich to grow even more, straining up against his flat belly and furry brown pubes that formed a soft wreath around his girth. She stroked his shaft and gripped his nutsack and rubbed the sticky tip of his penis against her lips and on her cheeks.

The soft warm breath from her mouth was like a feather stroking the head of his cock. She gripped his balls firm and her hand flew back and forth on his shaft until he exploded, his semen showering her tits with a lovely pearl necklace. The two had cleaned up in the shower together afterwards and for the first time, Rich's fingers slid inside her sex as she moaned. He rubbed her pussy lips and clit until she shuddered against him a second time. They dried off and lay in front of the fireplace, Ruby's fingers stroking Rich's chest hair and then down to his pubes. Their kisses were deep and perfect. His leaking penis made pre-cum trails glisten on his belly until her soft touches finally caused another eruption of thick cum from his swollen member.

"I love your dick," she whispered. "It's amazing to watch it explode like that. It's wonderful."

"It is, when you're around," Rich said.

THE NEXT week, Rich found a hastily scrawled message on the windshield wiper of his car. He stood in the parking lot of the Lola Tilly Commons, his hands shaking.

"You still owe us. We won't go away. Either pay up or you and the bitch will be sorry."

Rich racked his brain trying to figure out the threat. It took the better part of the day before it hit him like a log truck with burnt out brakes. When he was still on the crab boat, he had gone to a poker game with some of the other guys. That night, he couldn't lose. All the stars aligned and he kept winning. On top of it, it was like he knew what the others had in their hands. He hadn't paid attention at first, but then he realized the shiny tiled wall behind the men was reflecting their hands back to him. Halfway through the game, he had finally realized what he was really seeing. After that, he really could do no wrong.

In the end, he had taken home over $5000 and the men from the crab boat had been furious. He shrugged it off and figured they would cool down and just chalk it up to a bad gambling day. Apparently, they didn't. Now, months later, they wanted their money back. But it was all gone, spent on his truck, his college tuition, some bills, and a few new things for himself. He fretted about the threatening note for a couple of days, feeling himself distant from Ruby in class and daydreaming through his work at Fred Meyer. But by the time the weekend was rolling around again, all he could think of was Ruby and maybe this would be the weekend he will finally lose his virginity.

Rich planned a big weekend for the two of them. He rented a cabin out at Skinny Dick's Halfway Inn, one with a hot tub and everything. He picked Ruby up at 6:00 PM and they had a nice dinner at The River's Edge. They made it to the cabin around 8:30. Since it was summer, it was still bright outside. They checked in, pleased that they were the only visitors at the lodge it appeared, except for the trucks they saw parked around the bar. Rich grabbed their bags and hurried inside. Ruby loved the rustic cabin and within ten minutes, Rich was in his underwear on the bed, wrapped up in Ruby's arms. Her kisses were deep and warm and his desire grew long and hard in his shorts, peeking out the top of the elastic band.

Neither Ruby nor Rich heard the door to the cabin slowly open. In fact, it wasn't until the acrid smell of the filthy chloroform soaked rag smothered the consciousness from him that he knew anything was wrong at all. When he woke up, he found himself on the floor in front of the fireplace. His hands were bound behind his back. His head throbbed and he tasted blood and something else in his mouth. His eyes were unfocused but a sharp slap to the side of his face brought them clear. He stared into the face of Buck Edwards. With him, Dale Hooper and Steve McCandless came into view as well. He tried to move, but Dale held him down along with Steve while Buck stood in front of him.

He was naked from the waist down, his flannel shirt not covering this thick uncut penis that stood out straight from his beer gut. Fear filled Rich and he twisted his head around back and forth and finally saw Ruby. She was sitting in a straight-back chair in her baby blue panties. Thick nylon rope bound her to the chair. Her breasts stuck out from between the ropes. Her eyes were wide with terror and her face was a swollen damp wreck, hair matted to her brow. A thick rag was stuffed in her mouth as a gag, held in place by a strip of duct tape.

"I told you we would get ours one way or the other," Buck said moving close to Rich's face. The man pulled away but Buck held his head still by gripping a handful of hair while he smacked him in the face with his thick penis. "Looks like you spent all that scratch. Well that's okay. We like ass too. Figured your lady here will enjoy watching us give you the ride of your life." Rich pulled and writhed, trying to move away from Buck, but the other men held him still.

"Sorry I busted your lip a bit when we came in here," Buck said touching the sensitive wound on Rich's lip causing him to pull away. "But that sure didn't slow you sucking down that nut. Damn, kid. You can suck the chrome off a bumper."

Rich's eyes grew large as he realized what he was tasting in his mouth. He glued his lips together in a tight line as Buck's penis traced along his lips, pressing hard against them.

"You might as well relax, Bucko. It's gonna be a long night. Steve here already fed you his load. You licked it up like a starvin' calf."

Rich looked at Ruby whose eyes poured tears anew. She closed her eyes as Buck's cock slid inside Rich's mouth, gagging him. Soon, Dale changed places and his thick, stubby uncut dick slid into Rich's wet mouth, his thick crop of black pubes pressing suffocatingly into Rich's nose. Rich heard Buck spit into his hand and then felt his rough, thick fingers probe his anus. Rich looked into Ruby's face as the man's cock split him in half, his mouth opening in a silent scream, tears stinging his eyes, as Dale continued to thrust his prick deep inside his mouth. Buck plowed into Rich's ass until he was balls deep, gripping the man's shoulders and then starting a hard and steady fuck in and out of his ruined hole. Rich saw Ruby turn her face away as Buck's brutal rape continued and then he knew no more.

When Rich awoke, he lay on the bed, his head in Ruby's lap. He tried to raise up, but the pain in his neck and shoulders, not to mention his asshole was blinding.

"Don't try and move. Just rest for now," she said with tenderness. Rich looked around the room frantically. "They're gone. They said if we tell, they'll come back and do the same to me while you watch…and then kill us both," Ruby added with a flat certainty that seemed to say volumes without uttering a single word. "I still think we should call the police."

Rich sat up, wincing in pain. "Baby, I know, but please. I would be so embarrassed. Let's just try and forget it."

"Not that easy to forget your boyfriend eating cock all night long while he takes it up the ass over and over. Part of me thinks that isn't the first time you'd been fucked."

"What? No, that's not true. I've never done anything like that. I'm sorry it happened and even sorrier you saw it, but can't we just find a way to…"

"Every time I close my eyes, I see one of them sliding their dick into your mouth and ass. I lost count how many times they fucked you."

"I don't care, just as long as they didn't touch you."

"Well, I care. You were pure. You were mine. Now, you're dirty and ruined," Ruby began to sob.

Rich sat forward and tried to put his arms around her. "Don't! You smell like them. You smell like shit and cum," she pulled away and ran to the other side of the room. Rich sat stunned like a wounded puppy, his mind reeling. Finally, he got up and went to the bathroom and climbed in the shower and tried to wash away the stains along with the shame.

NATHANIEL'S HEART broke with the story. The cruelty and injury were so profound he found himself staring at the big, burly man that had somehow shrunk in size. Rich's gaze was vacant and hurt as he stared out at the endless road before them.

"Don't know why I told you all that. Shit. I've never told a soul. Only Ruby knows about it. I'd die if my guy friends knew I'd been raped like a whore."

Nathaniel felt the palpable sadness fill up the empty spaces in the conversation. "So, what happened next, Rich? For you and Ruby."

"Well it kind of all fell apart. We tried to keep dating but she just cringed every time I touched her. She cried and pulled away. Even after some months, she would only kiss and let me play with her titties. I still was waiting, hoping that it would get better. Finally, probably just in desperation, I went to a whorehouse. I just wanted to fuck someone, you know? I was so tired of waiting and wondering. I went out to Skinny Dick's again. Went into the bar and had a beer and asked the bartender guy if there were any ladies free for the night. He said sure and this older woman came and sat by me in a few minutes. She was nice and kind, slid her hand into my lap and rubbed my dick, but nothing happened. She told me to come with her and we went to her cabin. She had me undress and she started sucking my dick. It felt really great, but I was like a limp noodle. She even got naked and tried to stuff my poor dick up her shaved puss, but finally, she just stopped. She lay beside me and proceeded to tell me it was okay if I liked boys, telling me plenty of other big tough guys like me preferred dick to pussy. I was so destroyed, I just got dressed and drove away."

"That sounds exceedingly difficult," Nathaniel said, reaching over to grip Rich's shoulder. Rich looked at his hand and then into his face like he was going to say something, but in the end, he just kept driving while Nathaniel rubbed his shoulder and neck in a kindly gesture. Rich sighed.

"Anyway, that was three years ago. Ruby and me, we still talk and even hang out. She kind of did like me and tried to go on other dates. But in the end, she still just can't get over it all. I get so lonely sometimes, I even take off for Anchorage for the weekend or something and check out Craigslist ads and just hook up with guys. I don't even really like it, but for some reason, I still get hard when a guy forces me to suck his dick or fucks me. I don't know why. It's like that thing broke me. I mean, I think it's great for guys to fall in love or be all queer with each other. I don't have a problem with it. But at the end of the day, I really want to be a straight guy with a girl who loves fucking her. That's what I want. I always wanted that until those assholes did that shit to me. Now, it's all I feel like I can do."

"And Ruby?" Nathaniel asked.

"She runs a coffee shop in Delta. She mostly does good. Plenty of guys ask her out, even some girls I've heard. But I don't think that's what she wants either. It's just so fuckin' unfair, you know? She was the one for me and those bastards took it away."

The truck rounded a corner and the lights of the town came into view. "Speaking of Delta, it's right there ahead of us. You got a place to stay, buddy?" Rich asked.

"I do not," Nathaniel answered.

"Well I'm probably an idiot. Probably will end up with my throat cut or your dick up my ass, but why don't you just come bunk at my place for now? Not that many places to stay in this town."

"I would be very grateful."

Rich pulled his truck into the parking lot behind a warehouse on the edge of town and uncoupled from the trailer and took off toward his home. He parked in front of a small A-Frame house surrounded by Black Spruce. He grabbed his duffel bag from the back and climbed down from the cab. Nathaniel followed him into the house. It was freezing cold and dark. The air hung stale and still in the freezing house.

"I'll get the lights on and check everything out, then I'll get a fire going."

"Leave the fire to me," Nathaniel said.

"Okay, thanks. Um, wood and kindling there," Rich pointed to the small door beside the big rock fireplace. You can even use a starter log if you want."

"I will be fine. Go ahead and do your other tasks."

Rich looked perplexed at the dark man but finally shrugged and went toward the back of the house. He needed to turn the water on and get the hot water heater turned up as well. He felt oddly peaceful about having this stranger in his home. He was so tired of being alone. Honestly, if the guy ended up being gay and crawling into his bed tonight, he would almost welcome the company and the sex.

Nathaniel took the logs and kindling and arranged them in a huge tower of wood. He reached down and took a match and struck it against the stone and simply held it to the edge of one of the logs. Instantly, the stack of firewood blazed bright, like a Viking pyre, pushing the darkness and cold out of the room. Rich came back into the room wearing his shirt but no pants, totally amazed at the roaring fire.

"Holy shit. I was just getting ready to change and I saw the glow from the fire. I thought you might have set the place on fire it was so bright. Fuck me, you know how to start a fire," Rich said with a big, crooked smile.

Nathaniel grinned. "I've learned a few things about it. Should warm the place up pretty soon. Feel free to continue with your changing. You might want to take a long shower."

"Thanks. Um, what I kind of had in mind. But don't worry. Lots of hot water. You can take a nice one too. I bet you need to piss or take a nice long shit. Well, if you do, I'll just leave the door unlocked. Feel free. Won't bother me."

"Thank you. I will come eliminate my waste in a few moments."

Rich shook his head. "Dang, you are one odd duck."

He pulled his shirt off and padded down the hall toward the bathroom. The heat from the living room was already knocking the chill off the bathroom. Rich turned on the shower and let the large walk-in stall fill with steamy warmth. He loved this shower. It was one of the best parts of the house. He had jerked off so many times thinking of Ruby and him, wet and slick in the water, fingers exploring one another's secret spots. He slid his underwear off and walked into the water cascading from the overhead rain shower, feeling the soothing warmth flow over his aching body. He soaped up his hairy chest with the shower gel and rubbed the lather into his stinky pits and down to his belly and crotch. His penis swelled as he worked the lather around the thick shaft until all seven inches stood proudly away from his legs, his heavy sack rolling in his fingers as he cleaned himself. He worked his way around to his furry ass crack and dug a finger up inside his fleshy knot, feeling the muscle relax and welcome the probing. He slipped a second finger inside and closed his eyes, imagining Ruby's thin fingers being up there.

He guessed most men didn't think a lot about their girlfriend finger fucking their ass, but to him, it was electric and sort of pushed reset on the whole ass rape thing.

Rich heard the bathroom door open and heard Nathaniel come in and begin pissing like a race horse. He took a peek out the opening of the shower and saw the man was standing naked in front of the toilet. His skin was tan and flawless. The round mounds of his glutes stood out like bowling balls of hard muscle. A dusting of dark hair feathered from the crack but otherwise, he was smooth and striking. Rich instantly felt intimidated. When Nathaniel turned around, Rich's eyes stared. His chest was hard and defined, a crop of black hairs stretched across. A thin line of fur ran down to his navel and then widened to a tight triangle of thick fur around a penis that was stunning to say the least. It hung heavy and long, easily more than eight inches long on top of plum-sized testicles that rode low and loose in his scrotum. His legs were muscled and solid, covered with fine hairs that thickened from his knees to his feet. Nathaniel looked up into Rich's face with an unfathomable gaze.

"When you finish, I would enjoy bathing," he said in that low, sultry voice that flowed like melted butter and brown sugar. His hands hung loose at his sides. He put his weight on one leg making him look like a statue. Rich swallowed and continued to stare.

"Um, you can get in now," he said, reaching for a towel to cover up his body that felt misshapen and doughy, not to mention his dick that was beginning to swell. Nathaniel smiled and walked past him and stood under the water, raising his hands and feeling the shower flow over him as if he had never felt it before in his life. The water clung in tiny droplets on his thick eyelashes and nose and on the light dusting of hairs on his chest.

"You can use the shower gel or soap or whatever if you want," Rich offered, wondering for a moment if the man had literally never taken a shower before in his life. Nathaniel gripped the gel and squirted a palm full into his hand and rubbed it over his body, smiling at the sensation of his hands gliding over his skin.

Rich felt his dick swell even more and turned to leave. He had to get out the bathroom and clear his head. He went to the kitchen and grabbed a beer out of the fridge and stood in front of the fire feeling the warmth sink into his skin and dry the beads of water from his back and belly and hair. He kept trying to figure it out. There was something oddly comforting about having this total stranger in his house. Normally, something like this would have unnerved him, brought back dangerous memories. But instead, it felt relaxed and calming. Something about this weirdo was like wrapping up in a downy soft blanket. He seemed both ancient and childlike at the same time. Rich stared into the fire, watching the flames dance against the walls of his house. The empty place in his heart seemed even bigger tonight. He closed his eyes. The ache for Ruby was overwhelming. He sighed and hugged himself, feeling miserable and somehow comforted at the same time. He felt a presence behind him and turned. Nathaniel stood behind him, dripping on the floor. He had a curious smile as if he knew a secret and was dying to tell it. His naked body glowed copper in the flicker of the fire. For a moment, it almost seemed as if large chestnut wings spread out behind him.

"You want some shorts or something buddy? I mean, damn, if I looked as good as you I'd walk around naked all the time too."

"Does my presence offend you?"

"Uh, no. Kind of the opposite, you know. Kind of giving me a chub here, brother. Remember all the shit I told you in the truck?"

"You mean how you are sometimes attracted to males?"

"Yeah. Like that. Probably a little easier for me if we keep being naked a little on the DL."

"DL? I infer you mean you prefer I be dressed. In that case, yes. I could use some other garments."

"You talk so weird, buddy. Hey you know what? Fuck it." Rich pulled the towel off and dropped it to the floor. "We can just be all natural tonight."

Nathaniel looked at him and stared again into his face. "Your penis is erect. Would you rather I be erect too?"

"No, that's not necessary. I just get boned up real easy, especially when I am naked. But if you get some wood, don't worry. I won't be offended or anything."

Nathaniel smiled and looked at Rich's beer. "Might I bother you for a drink? I appear to be very thirsty."

"Oh shit. Of course. Come on in here and I will show you the kitchen. Would you like something to eat? I probably could make us a sandwich or make some bacon and eggs. Here's a beer." He handed the glass bottle to the tall man, popping off the top as he did. The stranger took a long drink and then stared at the bottle.

"Curious. This drink appears to have an intoxicating effect."

"Yeah. That's the point, you know? So bacon and eggs, okay?" Nathaniel nodded, continuing to drink. He walked over to a bar stool and sat down, his naked legs almost touching the ground he was so tall. Rich grabbed an apron and tied it around his waist. "Don't normally cook naked. Better wear this or I'll fry my dick as well as the bacon."

Nathaniel watched Rich move around the kitchen, deftly laying the bacon in the pan. The smoky smell filled his nostrils and made his mouth water. Rich opened a package of frozen biscuits and placed four of them on a baking sheet in the hot oven. He grated up a couple of potatoes he found and sizzled them in a cast iron skillet of oil until they were crispy and brown. He cracked four eggs and fried them up in the bacon grease. When the biscuits were done, he slathered them with great dollops of butter and put them on plates along with the bacon, eggs, and hash browns. Rich grabbed another couple of beers from the fridge and sat down on a bar stool beside the dark, quiet man.

"Hope you're hungry, buddy," Rich said with a smile. He held up his beer bottle toward Nathaniel in a toast. The tall man held his bottle up and Rich reached over and tapped the long neck with his bottle. "Cheers, Mate," he said.

Nathaniel watched Rich dig into the food and followed suit. He forked up a large amount of hash browns and tasted. His eyes closed as the flavor of the crispy fried potatoes filled his mouth. He reached for a piece of bacon and bit it, allowing it to crumble and mix along with the potatoes. He then cut into the egg and watched the bright yellow yolk flow, scooping up the hot flavors and pushing them into his fork with the edge of his biscuit the way he watched Rich. He closed his eyes again and savored the explosion of flavors in his mouth. He felt his belly rumble as the food slid down his throat. It was the most amazing sensation he had ever experienced. No wonder so many people ate far more than they needed. The sensation was intoxicating like the beer, he thought.

"Taste okay to you?" Rich asked, swallowing a big bite.

"This food is quite delectable. I believe it is, what do you say, my favorite?"

"Well great. I always love eating breakfast food no matter what time of the day. Damn, buddy. I know you are enjoying the food but that's the first time I saw a plate of eggs and bacon give a dude a woody!" Rich said with a laugh.

Nathaniel looked down to his lap and noticed his erection. "Yes, it is profoundly pleasing me, no doubt."

"Shit, that is one impressive cock, buddy."

"Thank you, I enjoy the sensation of an erection." Nathaniel said with a full mouth.

"Yeah, you and every man and boy on the planet. One of God's greatest gifts."

"It is a great gift from the Creator. There is no doubt of that."

The men finished their meal and cleared the plates and pans away, taking turns washing up and putting the dishes away. Rich hung up his apron and instantly felt more naked. Nathaniel continued to feel utterly at home in his own skin. He went to the living room and sprawled his long frame on one of the couches in front of the fire, now blazing with so much heat it was almost hot. Rich thought of turning on the television, but he just wasn't in the mood for news or reality shows. He stretched and rubbed his eyes. The momentary enjoyment of the food and friendly, albeit strange, conversation had been a welcome respite. But now the melancholy that he had been living in for so long descended around him like an old flannel shirt that you had worn so many times it felt like a second skin.

"Hey, Nathaniel. I'm pretty tired, so I think I'll head to bed. If you want to stay out here, there's a quilt and even some sheets in that cedar chest over there. If you would rather come back and sleep in my room, the bed's pretty big. It won't bother me or nothing."

Nathaniel reached up and gripped Rich's hand, his gaze seemingly penetrating the sorrowful exterior and reaching deep within him. "I will come lie with you. I would like to pray and meditate for a time before I come and join you. Will that please you?"

"Sure, buddy. That sounds good. For some reason I don't really want to sleep alone tonight." Nathaniel's grip was hot and electric. It felt like a glove of static electricity that didn't dissipate. The vibration and charge just continued to thrum and throb against Rich's hand. It sent a bolt of encouragement into his soul somehow and he found himself actually smiling.

"Wow, you are full of surprises," Rich said, sliding his hand from Nathaniel's big grip. He padded down the hall, took a quick piss and brushed his teeth, and headed for the bed. He opened his drawer to take out a pair of underwear and then just closed it. He normally slept in the raw, he wasn't going to change just in case Mr. Oddball crawled in with him. He was so conflicted, he didn't know what to think anyway. More than half of him hopes he ended up on the receiving end of that amazing cock. The other part just wanted a friend to be close and caring. "God, I am so fucked up," Rich whispered to the dark as he turned on his side away from the door and tried to sleep.

Back in the living room, Nathaniel slipped to the floor and sat crossed-legged in front of the fire and opened his hands and palms on his knees in an intercessory gesture. He closed his eyes and felt the warmth of the fire on his skin. He loved the full feeling in his belly and the sensuousness of the food. He could feel Rich's sadness and desire emanating from the bedroom down the hall.

"Father, Creator. Show me Your will for Rich. I want to be an instrument of healing and comfort to his hurting heart. Show me the path to do the same for Ruby. Fill me with Your purpose and creative love." He lifted his hands to the ceiling and the large chestnut wings unfurled again, the copper feathers like burnished bronze in the orange glow of the fireplace. As the supplication rose to the heavens, Nathaniel felt the whisper of the Creator in his mind. A smile grew across his face as a single tear slid from his eye. He was alive once again. "Om Shanti," he chanted.

Rich felt the mattress sink down as Nathaniel slid under the covers in the bed. The man lay still beside him for a while, then he turned on his side and spooned close behind. Rich's heart began to beat wildly as the man's arms enveloped him, pulling close. Nathaniel's face rested on the back of Rich's head. Rich reached up and gripped the man's large hands, sinking back against him as their heartbeats synchronized. Rich adjusted his legs, parting them slightly, feeling Nathaniel's swollen member slide up against his ass crack and against his soft furry sack. He held his breath, waiting for the pressure, the pain when the man penetrated him. But instead of the familiar sensation, he felt the pressure of the man against his back, pressing so hard it began to feel as if he were slipping inside. His eyes were closed, prepared.

He adjusted his back, reaching down and gripping his knee, pulling his legs farther apart and in that moment, a scream almost forced its way out of his mouth as the man behind him slid inside his entire body in one fluid movement. He was penetrated body and soul. His heart slid in beside Rich's own pounding cardiac muscle. In that moment, the men shared the same space, the same breath, the same broken heart. Rich felt his own hands lift up and grip his face, but then again, it wasn't his hands. It was his strange friend, ministering healing and grace.

Rich found himself weeping, his sorrow and pain pouring forth like a fountain. The men were linked tighter than steel. Their molecules vibrated and shared the same thoughts and sensations. The sad and damaged part of Rich's mind began to open and feel restored, like a healing oil had been poured out. Rich found his pulse pick up even more. His passion and desire grew to a flame and wave after wave of sexual quickening shattered through him, like a machine gun of orgasms, again, and again, and again until he lay limp and spent.

When Rich woke, he was alone. He rose and moved through the house looking for Nathaniel, yet somehow knew he would not find him. He looked around and realized for the first time in months, he felt hopeful. He touched his face and tried to recall the unbelievable experience of last night. How could you experience something so intimate and sensual without actually getting fucked? It was more than fucking, it was transcendent. He realized his dick was rock hard and straining up against his belly. He stood in the middle of the living room and wrapped his fist around his penis and stroked the soft flesh, feeling his desire climb and explode in a thick fountain of semen. He opened his eyes to the brightness of the light outside, feeling his cum sticky between his fingers as he rubbed his belly.

"Damn," he whispered with a smile.

RUBY TUNED the radio to XM 31 and the soft sounds of the Coffeehouse station filled the cold air with strumming guitars. She switched on the strings of white twinkle lights strung between the beams and the bright glow made her smile. She had felt so bad lately, God, forever it seemed. Every day since that horrible night at Skinny Dicks had been as black as the next for the most part. She tried to bury herself in work and school, but the hole was still there. She had taken up baking and filled the coffee shop with fresh baked goods until there were so many she needed to throw them out. She tried to spend a lot of time with her little niece, but that seemed hollow as well. She stayed away from her parents as much as possible since that was an instant trip to guilt and depression-land. In her mother's mind, whatever had happened between Rich and her was clearly her fault. Her mother adored Rich. Her dad felt the same. In fact, it almost was weird how close the two men had become. They had been fishing and hunting a number of times. She lost count how often the two had met at The Cave for a drink. Even after everything fell apart, the two of them managed to keep in touch until finally she supposed Rich just gave up.

It was still mostly the same: she closed her eyes and she saw Rich bent over, sucking a dick while one of those monsters penetrated his ass, plowing him like a cheap whore. And no matter how she tried to rationalize it, it always seemed like Rich didn't put up a fight or tried to stop it. He just submitted like a scared boy or a whipped dog that knew he was going to lose the fight anyway. She could not figure out why she didn't feel pity or compassion for him. Instead, she just felt embarrassment and disgust. She was a naturally very caring person but those evil trolls had robbed her of all that. She was a zombie, hollow and she simply didn't know how to love anymore.

She had fought against all the setups and blind dates for weeks and months after that night. The last thing she wanted was to stick her toe back in the river. After many months, she finally accepted one of the offers to go out and headed out to Clearwater Lodge for drinks and dinner. Jared was a good guy, local boy who had always carried a torch for her. They had fumbled around together in the back of his car a few times in high school. He had shown her the first erect penis she had ever seen other than her little brother who walked around the house in a constant state of arousal it seemed. She lost track of how many times his heavy dick had fallen out of his boxer shorts like a python dropping from a branch onto an unsuspecting prey. Jared had closed her hands around it and she had done her best to stroke the silky flesh as he instructed. Her eyes had widened as his breath increased and she watched the pearly white spurt of semen shoot from his cock and splash in thick blobs on his black T-shirt. She had felt herself grow wet as she stroked him and loved the feeling of power it gave her as she watched Jared slump back spent and vulnerable.

She had enjoyed visiting with Jared, catching up and just feeling like a person again. He was kind and funny. Thankfully, he wasn't all touchy-feely either. No one said anything but it was like he was out on a date with a time bomb that could go off at any moment.

"You look really nice tonight, Ruby," Jared said pouring more wine into Ruby's glass. She smiled.

"Thanks, Jared. It's been a while since someone said that to me."

"How's the coffee shop doing?"

"Um, pretty good. You know, I've got my regulars and as summer comes on, more vacationers are coming through town."

"Yeah, I like the way you fixed the place up."

Ruby smiled. The small talk was excruciating but she appreciated Jared's effort. He reached across the table and took her hand.

"I hate seeing you so sad, Ruby. I wish I could help make it better," he said, rubbing his thumb across her hand. It wasn't creepy or off-putting. She could tell he genuinely cared. But something in his eyes also let her know he was still a horny guy. She drank more wine and smiled again, softly pulling her hand away to grab some bread.

"I'm going to hit the head. Be right back."

She nodded. Ruby noticed when Jared stood, a large lump pressed against his slacks. She liked seeing that but it also caused her to feel embarrassed. She made it through the dinner and enjoyed the talk and the company. When Jared took her home, he reached over and held her hand. It was sweet and dopey, but she admired the effort and was glad he was trying to be so sweet. As he pulled up at her house, Ruby felt her stomach contract. She knew what was next and she dreaded it. Part of her wanted to run to the door, slam it, and just be done with this evening. Another part liked feeling alive for a change and wondered what it would be like to let someone into her life again. They stood on the front porch and Jared stood close. He took Ruby in his arms and pulled her close. It felt nice to have strong arms around her again. Ruby could feel Jared's strong heart beat against her chest as he held her close. She lifted her face up and his lips tenderly touched hers. His breath was warm and sweet. Thank God he didn't just start stabbing his tongue inside hers. God, how she hated that, she thought. She felt his cock press against her leg and she thought, well that didn't take very long. She held his face in her hand and returned his kisses, enjoying the tingles that she felt between her legs as well.

"Would you like me to come in and stay a while?" he asked.

"Sure," Ruby said with timid sincerity.

She went to the fridge and brought back a couple of beers. Jared built a fire and they sat on the couch drinking. She allowed his hands to brush against her breasts as he continued to kiss her. She liked the feel of his hands there. She unbuttoned his shirt and ran her fingers across his mostly smooth chest, enjoying he feel of his nipples hardening as she touched them. She reached behind her back and unfastened her bra and pulled her sweater over her head along with her bra and lay back on the couch pillows, her skin glowing bright in the firelight. Jared smiled and pulled his shirt off and stood up and pulled off his trousers as well. His boxer briefs were tented out, a thick trail of dark fur ran from his navel into his shorts. He reached down and slid his fingers into the waistband of Ruby's pants and slid them off her hips. She lay back with her legs parted, her black panties lacy and soft against her creamy white belly. Jared reached and touched the soft folds of skin underneath the panties. Ruby gasped and felt herself grow wet as the man's fingers traced the lips of her pussy.

Jared leaned close and his lips and tongue began to tease and play with her nipples as he continued to rub her damp sex. Ruby felt her legs spread wider as Jared's fingers slid inside the side of her panties and began to rub and probe inside her vulva. She took his hand and moved his fingers up to her clitoris, which seemed to be completely foreign territory to Jared. She moved his fingers in a circle and closed her eyes as his touch built the passion within her. She thrust her hips up against his hand, which unfortunately gave Jared the idea that she wanted him to pull her panties off. He stopped playing with her clit and pulled her panties off and buried his face in her wetness. His tongue licked and lapped but somehow missed her special spot. He gripped her hips and thrust his tongue in and out of her mound like a tiny wet penis.

Before she knew what was happening, Jared was leaning up and kissing her hard with wet, sticky lips that tasted of beer and pussy. His fingers probed her vulva and slid deep within. She gasped and tried to pull away. He pressed harder and Ruby felt the tip of his penis press against her vagina like a snake looking for a hole. Her eyes flew open and she gripped his shoulders and pushed him off with all her might. The look on his face was a mixture of anger and surprise for a moment as he pushed against her again, this time the head of his dick penetrating her.

"No!" Ruby yelled and pushed and then reached down and gripped Jared's balls in a tight twist that caused him to gasp and moan. He fell to the floor holding his junk.

"Oh shit. I think you ruptured a nut. Fuck me!" he moaned.

Ruby scrambled to her feet and grabbed a blanket from the back of the couch, wrapping it around herself as she backed toward her bedroom.

"I'm sorry. I'm sorry. I just can't," she said through tears. Jared laid back on the rug, eyes wide; his erection slowly deflating until his penis lay soft against his thick brown bush.

"I thought you wanted to," he whispered clutching his scrotum again.

"I know. I did too. I just can't. Can you just go?"

Jared stood up, his naked form glowing bright in the light of the fireplace. "I'm gonna have black and blue balls after this," he said muttering to himself. As he pulled his underwear and slacks on, he added, "You need to figure your shit out, Ruby." He grabbed his shirt and shoes and stomped from the house. Ruby slid down to the floor and wept.

That was the last time she had tried to connect with a man. She had two flirtatious encounters with a girlfriend from UAF since. Hannah was funny and sweet and never made her feel threatened. When they would cuddle on the couch, it felt safe and relaxing. At night, when Hannah would crawl between her legs and lick her clitoris until she came in throbbing waves, she smiled and luxuriated in the sensation. But in the end, it still wasn't what her heart wanted. She wanted Rich. She wanted his strong arms and his sweet, country boy face close to hers. She wanted his furry butt and thick hairy legs. She wanted the feel of his chest and belly against hers. But when she thought of trying again, the fear gripped her and she felt icy fingers of dread clamp around her heart. The only joy she had at all was sliding her fingers into her own pussy and clit and masturbating to the thought of his sweet face and warm smile.

Ruby looked up as the bell on the door chimed. It was still so early. She was just about to tell the person that she wouldn't be open for another hour until she saw him. Once she did, she totally forgot about everything else.

The tall man stood in the doorway looking like he had just walked out of a dream. His shoulder-length hair was full of soft curls, blowing in the early morning breeze. His shoulders were wide and strong. She looked at the shirt unbuttoned midway down his chest and saw a fine dusting of black hair. His legs were thick and strong, feet huge in big black boots. But as she looked back at his face, the eyes stole her soul. They were so deep they seemed to have no end. His smile was gentle and yet filled her with desire.

"I hope it's not too early," he said with a rich musical voice that resonated inside her head.

"Uh, no. It's fine. What can I get you?"

"I am unfamiliar with this beverage," he said strangely. "But I would like to experience it. Do you have a suggestion of what I should try?"

Ruby smiled at the utter ridiculousness of the statement. "Okay. Well, how about a nice Vanilla Mocha. You would probably really like that."

"I will look forward to it. Thank you."

Ruby worked her magic with the espresso machine and foamed the milk and poured the concoction together like a secret potion. She handed the rich, steaming mug to the stranger. He took the cup and took a long drink of the hot coffee, closing his eyes as he swallowed as if he had never tasted anything like it in his life.

"So, how is it?" she asked.

"It is quite astonishing. I am pleased."

"Well good. Um, that's $4 unless I can get you something else."

"I do not have any currency. Perhaps I could work for you to pay for this beverage."

Ruby frowned. Of course, this dreamy guy was also a deadbeat. She sighed.

"Forget it," she said. As she turned to go back behind the counter, the man gripped her hand. She was momentarily frightened but as his hand tightened around her, she found herself staring into his eyes, feeling like he was peering into her very heart.

"You are so sad. You are hurt and lonely. You long for your love, but are afraid to try again."

"How can you know..?"

"Let me stay and work with you today. Let me help you," he said as more of a command than a suggestion. She nodded.

"Alright. You can wash up and clear the tables. I'll show you how to do some other things later on. Here's an apron," she handed the bright green apron to the man who held it, seemingly with no idea of what it was for. Ruby wrapped the apron around his slim waist and tied it in the front. There was some kind of amazing energy that radiated from this tall stranger. She should have been freaked out, running for the hills. Instead, she felt a sense of calm and safety she had rarely ever felt.

As the morning wore on and customers flooded into the shop, she was struck by how at ease the normally wary locals were of this odd man. He had casual conversations with so many, gently touching them on the back or shoulder almost in some kind of blessing. He cleared tables and washed the dishes. Ruby showed the man how to operate the espresso and cappuccino machines and he seemed to intuitively understand without any additional instruction. By the end of the morning rush, he was taking orders, making coffee, and spreading his charm to the men and women that walked into the shop. In the lull before lunch, Ruby walked over to the man and gently touched his shoulder. She felt a jolt of energy pass between them.

"Thanks for today. You are an amazing worker. Everyone seems to really be taken with you. Um, I don't even know your name."

"Nathaniel."

"Nice. Uh, I probably should be paying you. You are helping me way more than a $4 coffee."

"There is no need. However, I could use a place to stay for a day or so. I am glad to continue to help you here if that will compensate you."

"I have a spare bedroom. You can just stay with me," she found herself saying before she even realized what she was doing. It was crazy that she would offer this total stranger a place to stay at her home and yet, there was no fear, no second guessing. She knew this man would never hurt her.

"I am grateful."

The two worked in concert the rest of the day. Rarely had Ruby felt so energized and happy. Nathaniel worked tirelessly and continued to meet and greet customers with warmth and sincerity, leaving each one smiling and comforted as they left the shop. In fact, she had seen at least six patrons return later in the day. Mostly women, but Carl Bishop from the hardware store seemed particularly taken with Nathaniel. Ruby watched as Nathaniel handed the man his coffee and gripped the man's hand briefly. Carl's eyes had widened and a peaceful, almost satiated look crossed his face. Ruby blushed when she saw the large burly man walk to the bathroom with an obvious boner pressing hard against his jeans. She didn't want to think about what he was doing in there for so long either.

Right before the two closed up for the day, the bell sounded again and Ruby felt her heart almost stop as Rich walked in the door. His casual smile and warm friendly charm exuding almost as much as Nathaniel's. He had stopped coming in the shop months ago. Ruby felt her pulse racing as he neared the counter.

"Mocha latte," he said with a grin. "How are you, Ruby?"

"I...I'm good, Rich. Nice to see you."

"I see this big lug has found his way to you," Rich said nodding toward Nathaniel who was sweeping.

"You know him?"

"I gave him a ride, picked him up almost to Barrow. Brought him down in the truck. Odd guy for sure but I really like him. So, he's working here?"

"Just for a few days. Wow, that's so strange, you two have met as well. He is a little weird but not in a bad way, you know?"

"I do know. He stayed with me last night. Was nice to have some company. I didn't know where he ran off to."

"He stayed with you? Um, I told him he could use my spare room tonight. Do you think I..?"

Rich's face darkened for a second, then he relaxed. "Normally, I would tell you that you were crazy. But with him, I know it's okay. Weird, huh?"

"I felt the same." Ruby handed Rich the latte and he put a $20 bill in her hand. As they touched, another jolt of energy seemed to arc between them. Ruby noticed Nathaniel looked over and was smiling.

"I'll get your change."

"No need. It's all for you. So nice to see you again, Ruby."

The woman looked up with eyes that sparkled with tears that begged to flow. "Yes it is."

"I'll see you, Ruby," Rich said taking his coffee. Rich nodded his head at Nathaniel, who waved with a wide grin on his face.

RUBY MADE spaghetti for dinner that evening and Nathaniel once again acted like it was the first time he had ever tasted pasta. Ruby poured a glass of merlot which Nathaniel marveled at. When she served a piece of cheesecake, the man acted like he was about to have an orgasm he was so moved.

"This is a remarkable experience," Nathaniel said. "My sensory faculties are overwhelmed."

Ruby shook her head thinking this guy is nuts. The two washed up and moved to the living room. Nathaniel sat beside her on the couch. The fire was blazing. Nathaniel had made the fire seemingly in a few seconds while she was out of the room. They sat staring at the fire, lost in thought. So seldom was Ruby at ease with silence like this when others were around. But tonight, she literally moved over and leaned against Nathaniel's strong shoulder, soaking in his amazing energy and peace. She barely moved as his arm, almost like a wing, wrapped around her in a loving gesture of security and safety.

"Your soul has been so hurt and damaged, Ruby. Your heart has grown fearful and cold. All you can see is the pain of the past and the horror of what happened to you and Rich. But there is healing. There is comfort. There is hope."

Tears splashed down on Ruby's face as Nathaniel spoke. She hated what he was saying. Part of her resisted it. But down deeper, something melted and cracked. She sobbed as a healing balm-like oil flowed through her.

"I'm too afraid. I want to love him again. I do love him, but I am so lost. All I can see is those men raping him."

"Let me take that away. Let me love you back to life," Nathaniel said with his deep soothing voice.

Ruby's mind reeled and her heart sped up. As she looked at the man, she felt like two people: one ready to run, hide, scream...the other ready to open up to this stranger and allow him to change her life.

Ruby whispered. "I'm still a virgin."

"And you shall remain," he said cryptically.

As Nathaniel's hands lightly touched Ruby's face, she felt her eyes close and she sank into a dream world. She saw the huge man stand in front of her. He was naked and almost glowed. His arms were outstretched and behind him, large chestnut wings with glowing ocher tips spread from behind him. She leaned back as he grew near. He gently spread her thighs and slid between them. As his face neared hers, the warmth and energy was almost unbearable. His lips brushed her eyes and nose, then found her lips and the sweet honey of his breath caused them to open.

They kissed long and deep, tongues touching and teasing. Ruby felt his strong hands caress her breasts, grip her smooth ass, and tenderly part her pussy and find her sensitive clit. His touch was like a thrumming vibrator that sent wave after wave of pleasure through her body. He moved his face to her sex and his tongue began to suck and tease her clit until her face flung back and she moaned in release as the man's strong hands gripped her trembling legs. She grabbed his long hair and thrust her sex hard against his face again and again as the orgasm continued. His finger teased her asshole, caressing the rosebud and slipping inside as she cried out in yet another orgasm.

Then she was in his arms, legs spread wide as she rode astride his sturdy hips. She could feel the tip of his cock pulsing against the lips of her vagina. She was so wet, she felt she was almost dripping. Slowly, deliberately, the man penetrated her pussy. His girth spread her lips wider than she had ever thought possible until she felt his balls pressed against her ass. There was no pain, no tearing, no fear. He slid his shaft out until only the head of his penis remained and then thrust deeply in again until she gasped, feeling his sack pound against her. She gripped his strong shoulders and rode his cock, thrusting it further and further within her wetness. Her breasts rocked and wiggled as she fucked herself harder and deeper on the man's huge member. Her head stretched back as she felt her climax building.

The man's breathing increased and a low growl began in his throat. She felt him shudder and shout as his seed blasted within her, causing her orgasm to explode in brilliant stars in her mind. He fucked deeper and deeper until it began to feel his entire body was sliding insider her. He felt his touch deep within her mind and heart. His warm seed flowed over her hurts. She cried and writhed as the tangled pain and horrors woven into her brain were pulled away, healing energy and love flowing into the scars left behind. And then, her vision filled with another face. Rich was there. He was inside her, fucking and filling her with all his love and care and her heart broke free in a torrent of desire and joy.

THE SUN was already streaming through the window when Ruby woke with a start. In Delta Junction in late May, this was most of the time but she sat up in a panic. She was in bed in a soft nightgown. Her hands moved involuntarily to her breasts and then between her thighs. Was it only a dream?

Across town, Rich sat up in bed breathing hard. He had just had the most intense dream of his life. He looked at the sheets and a large white stain of semen was decorating the fabric. His dick was still hard, the tip sticky with sperm. He hadn't had a wet dream since he was twelve. He could still remember the dream. He had been in the kitchen cooking a pork chop when he felt a hand on his back. He turned around to see Nathaniel in front of him. He was naked and behind him stretched vast wings the color of autumn leaves.

The large man gripped Rich by the shoulders and moved him close. His dark cinnamon colored eyes scorched into Rich's brain as his face and scratchy beard rubbed against Rich's face and his lips touched Rich's. The man's mouth felt welded to Nathaniel's, his warm breath filling his lungs. As the dark-haired man pressed his mouth hard against Rich's, it felt as if his entire face was beginning to meld with his own until it slipped inside. He felt the man's chest grow close with his and melt into his own. Nathaniel's cock pressed hard against Rich's penis and somehow it filled within him. With a rush, Rich's eyes flew open and he was back in bed.

Before he could realize what he was doing, he was driving toward town. He pulled up in front of the coffee shop and almost ran inside. Ruby was standing in the middle of the room, eyes moist and opened wide. He walked up to the woman and held his arms open. She looked at him, deep into his eyes, and to her it seemed she was looking into heaven. With trembling hands she reached out and pulled Rich's arms toward her and stepped into his embrace. Her face rose to meet his. He looked almost like he was shining in the early morning sunlight. His face lowered to hers and his lips touched hers, energy and power flowing from him to her. The sweetness of his kiss, the sensuous flick of his tongue she felt deep within her heart all the way down to her sex. She felt Rich's erection hard against her belly. She smiled, knowing her touch had caused that. Her hand slid down and gripped his shaft. He pulled away and smiled his crooked smile.

"What you got there, Ruby?"

"Not sure but I think I better unwrap it and see."

"Holy shit."

Ruby broke away from Rich's embrace and ran to the counter. She tore off a sheet of paper from a legal pad and grabbed a Sharpie and wrote:

Something came up. Closed today. See you all tomorrow. Thanks! XOXO

She taped the note to the door and pulled down the blinds just as Carl Bishop was getting out of his truck. The husky man just stared at the sign on the door like it was Chinese before he finally got back into his pickup and drove away.

Ruby gripped Rich by the hand and pulled him around the counter and into her small office. The room was tiny and cluttered, but was large enough for a soft couch that she often used for naps as well as a fluffy white faux-polar bear rug. She closed the door and turned on the lamp that filled the room with a soft golden light. Rich's eyes were wet as he pulled her close again, his lips almost touching hers.

"Oh honey," he sighed. "I'm so..."

Ruby's finger went up to his lips and pressed against them. "Shhhhh," she said. "It's all gone now. I have missed you, darling." The two embraced tightly, their faces pressed hard against each other. Ruby leaned close until her lips were lightly touching Rich's ear and whispered. "I'm going to fuck you now."

She pulled the bottom of Rich's t-shirt and ripped it up over his head and began to suck his nipples, rubbing his furry belly and chest. Her hands found his jeans and popped the button and ripped the zipper down, sliding them off his round ass. She gripped his white briefs and tugged them down underneath his large nutsack. She gripped his shaft and dove for his cock swallowing it until Rich's pubic bush tickled her nose. The sweet tang of his precum filled her mouth as she sucked him deep and hard, working his shaft and pulling off to bathe his large testicles in her mouth until the man was weak-kneed and gasping.

"Oh holy fuck. Oh God," he whispered.

Rich reached down and gripped Ruby's head and pulled her off his cock and kissed her deeply tasting himself on her tongue. He reached down and pulled her soft sweatshirt off, gripping her breasts in both hands. She pushed her pants down and stood in his arms naked and trembling as they kissed deeply. Rich stood on the bottom of his jeans and stepped out of them along with his shorts. He leaned Ruby over and laid her down on the soft white rug and slid down until his face was in her pussy. He turned around and felt Ruby's mouth envelop his penis and the two began to feast on each other's sex, licking, lapping, and sucking on one another until they were breathless and wet faced.

"I want you in my cunt now!" Ruby hissed.

"I don't have a condom."

"The hell with that. FUCK ME NOW!!"

Rich's eyes almost popped from his head as Ruby got on all-fours and presented her pussy like a bitch in heat. Rich crawled forward until the tip of his penis lay against her throbbing cunt, lips swollen with desire. He lined his dick up inside the wetness of her cunt and leaned forward, filling her tunnel in one slow motion until his belly rested against her.

Rich gripped Ruby's hips and pulled out and slid forward again. There was no pain or cry. His large member slid in and out of his sweetheart's pussy like a warm knife into a freshly baked cherry pie. Ruby gasped and spread her legs wider wanting more and more of her man inside her. Her vision was a cacophony of images, Rich and Nathaniel blurred in and out of focus. She was filled with one cock, then the other, now both. She was riding Rich's manhood like a wild horse, his stallion cock breeding her again and again, filling her desire and lust until her passion was ready to explode. With a final loud grunt, Rich thrust again and released his cum deep within Ruby's cunt. It pumped again and again filling her pussy with his seed until it leaked out the edges and flowed down her thighs. He flipped her around still inside her and kissed her deep and long, continuing to press his cock again and again inside her until she cried out in a lustful orgasm.

"Jesus, Mary, Joseph and Hot Fudge...I'm cummmming!" Ruby screamed, feeling her body explode in orgasmic desire throbbing around Rich's cock still buried deep inside her vagina.

The two lay in each other's arms, curled on the white rug. Ruby's head lay on Rich's arms. She ran her fingers through his chest hair down his belly to his pubes and playfully teased his penis as she felt his fingers play with her nipples and slide down between her legs and slide softly inside her pussy. Rich looked deep into her eyes.

"I feel like I've been dead and just came back to life," the man whispered into Ruby's ear. "I don't know how or why, I don't even care. You are all I ever wanted. Without you, I didn't care if I lived or died. You've been through so much. Oh honey, I can't believe…"

"Believe it, baby. It was a long, dark road filled with sadness and evil. But here we are. The moment we both dreamed about and waited for, we found each other again. I love you so much, baby," Ruby said, her lips finding Rich's lips again. "Take me home. I want you to make love to me again."

They dressed in a hurry and sped to Ruby's house. They ran inside, strewing clothes as they rushed to the bedroom. They stood at the foot of the bed, naked and holding hands like two young children. Rich leaned down and picked Ruby up in his arms and carried her to the bed. He lay between her legs and hugged her close, allowing their bodies to fit together as they kissed and rubbed their faces together. Ruby pulled her legs up and felt Rich's cock part her pussy lips and slide inside again.

The fullness and pressure of his sex inside her was intoxicating. His thick shaft filled her vagina and rubbed against her clit with every thrust. Her hands gripped his meaty, furry ass, her heels digging in like a jockey on a thoroughbred.

"Don't ever stop fucking me," she whispered as the man drove deep within her again and again. Sweat dripped from his face as he continued to plow her cunt, her wetness creating a slick road deeper and deeper into her.

"I'm...gonna...cummmmmm!" Rich roared as his ass slammed hard against Ruby and blasted his nut into her hungry sex. Ruby's head flew back and she screamed.

"Fuuuuck!" Her orgasm rocked through her in earthquakes of desire.

Unseen by either, a shadow large and dark poured from Rich's backbone and rose into the air like a silent, auburn cloud. The mist reassembled into Nathaniel's form. The large naked man ran his hands down his body, clothing himself in his dark garments and long, flowing coat. He smiled at the couple entwined on the bed and turned and disappeared.

Rich rose and pissed and went to the kitchen and returned with a bottle of chardonnay and a glass. He poured the wine and rested against the headboard of the bed, wrapping his arm around Ruby's small shoulders. They drank the wine and cuddled, watching the bright midday turn to softer late afternoon. When the wine was gone, Ruby sucked Rich's cock until it lay hard and flat against his belly again. Then she climbed onto Rich's solid belly and slipped his penis into her pussy again. She rode him like a cowboy, rocking her clit into his cock until she shouted with yet another orgasm. She pulled off and sucked Rich's cock and felt his semen jet into her mouth, gulping the thick, salty seed down her throat. She climbed up on his chest and kissed him. He grinned as his tongue tasted the sperm in her mouth.

"What made you do that?" Rich asked.

"I don't know. I just wanted to eat you up. You didn't mind, did you?"

"Nah. I mean, you know…" Rich blushed but his crooked smile spread across his face. "Not like I haven't tasted it before. Maybe we should get one of those strap-on dicks and you can really make me your bitch?"

Ruby giggled. "Maybe we will." She sucked her finger into her mouth and then slid it down his back between his meaty buns and wiggled around. She found the big man's asshole and slipped her wet finger inside. Rich sucked in his breath as she pressed deep against his prostate. "Just remember, Buddy. If you want something like this, your ass is mine. Get me one of those cocks and I'll fuck you silly." They collapsed in giggles and began kissing again.

Out on Highway 2, the tall man walked in long strides down the road toward Fairbanks. The wind whipped the man's coat and long hair as he walked along. A small smile crossed his face as he pictured Rich and Ruby wrapped up together in bed. He looked up to the blue sky and whispered a prayer of thanks to the Creator. He felt a sharp sting and burning on his shoulder. He stopped and pulled his coat sleeve down along with his t-shirt and stared at the new blue star that burned bright on his tan skin.

To be continued…

Here is a sample from another story you may enjoy:

Hot Gay Erotica

Shower
of Power

Angus MacGregor

THE SKY was streaked with orange and yellow ribbons by the time the engine crew made it back to headquarters. Ben and Colton had spent most of the trip cuddled up in the front of the cab. Jesse had pulled Brandon over to his side, his brown curls blowing against his face as they drove, his free hand rubbing the hard lump in the rookie's fire pants. Except for the occasional bump, Jesse had almost forgotten the big black rubber plug in his ass. As he shifted on the seat, the plug massaged his prostate again and again sending shudders through him and making his erection press hard against the fabric of his pants. He smiled thinking that he was actually enjoying the damn thing banging up on his magic spot like this.

Colton pulled into the compound and backed the engine into the garage bay. The guys secured the vehicle and got it ready for patrol tomorrow. When Colton passed him, the big blond man had fun gripping Jesse's ass and pressing the plug even deeper into his stretched anus, leaning over and whispering.

"Rookie, I can't wait to get inside your boy hole again."

Jesse smiled thinking that sounded pretty great to him as well. He and Brandon hobbled over to Jesse's truck and started to climb in. Ben came over.

"So, you boys just follow us over to our place. No need to head home first," he said.

"We figured we'd go home and clean up and everything," Brandon said. The truth was he just had to get the damn plug out of his hole and take a massive dump.

"Just come on over. You can clean up and take a big shit at our place, rookie," Ben said with a grin, reading Brandon's mind.

"Ok," Brandon answered with a laugh. "Hope your plumbing will be up to the task."

"Holy hell, if it can handle this farm boy's turds, it can handle whatever you have," Ben said heading back to Colton's truck. The men took off in a cloud of dust back toward town. Jesse pulled out and followed.

Brandon unfastened his pants and slid them down on his thighs. His penis was rigid, with thick veins standing out, a thin drop of precum oozing from the tip. "God, I can't wait to pull this damn plug out. I have been on the edge of cumming all afternoon," he said forlornly, looking down at his erection.

Jesse reached over and let his rough thumb rub against Brandon's dick head, rubbing against the precum and then sticking his thumb into his mouth to taste his buddy's honey. Brandon reached over and gripped the back of Jesse's neck and rubbed it tenderly. All he wanted was to jump in the shower with the big lug, or even better, soak in a tub, and go from there.

"Kind of funny, Ben and Colton asking us over and all, after being with us and inside us all afternoon. You would think they would be done with rookies for the day," Jesse said

"I get the idea they are gonna get back up inside us again, don't you?"

"Yeah, especially that Colton," Jesse said, remembering his big hands pressing on the plug in his ass.

"Yeah, that guy is maybe just a little bit too invested in your training," Brandon said with a snap. "He wants to rape your ass every time he looks at you."

"Ben was doing a pretty good number on your pussy himself," Jesse said half-heartedly. Even he knew Colton's attentions were more intense and romantic feeling than Ben's had been. There was definitely something real going on between him and Colton. But he also knew it was just sex, just some hot animal attraction, not something deeper. At least he didn't think so. He reached over and gripped Brandon's hand. Brandon looked at their hands and then up at Jesse and smiled. That touch, just like electricity again. His penis swelled as his thumb rubbed against Brandon's furry fingers.

The guys pulled into Ben and Colton's house about 10 minutes later. They both said, "Woah" when they saw the place. It wasn't huge, but it was beautiful. It was a two-story modern construction. Shake shingle siding that blended in beautifully with the forested surroundings. You could tell it was a new house and the rookies were eager to see inside.

They pulled off their boots and added them to the neat pile outside the front door. They stepped inside the cool front hallway that stretched all the way up to the second floor with a cool contemporary staircase leading upstairs. But their attention was taken away by what was in front of them. The entire back side of the house was glass and looked out on Mary's River. The water chattered and bubbled over mossy covered rocks and boulders as it flowed past the house. The kitchen, with its stainless appliances, looked sleek and modern. Comfortable sectional sofas made a U – shape in the living room. A large 60-inch LED television was mounted on the wall above the rock chimney and fireplace area. Usher was singing "Scream" over the sound system speakers that seemed to be in every room. Even though the volume was low, it was everywhere.

Just then Ben appeared from another room, probably the laundry room; he was still wearing his white briefs, but just that. Colton followed, wearing all of nothing at all. Colton stopped at the fridge and grabbed some beers, twisted off the caps, and handed them around. Jesse grabbed his and downed half of it in one chug. Colton did the same, grabbing Brandon in a big vice grip hug and pulled him close. The big man reeked of sweat and BO and one big whiff of his underarm was enough to make Brandon's cock swell to attention. Fuck this blond god, he thought.

"Glad you could come over and play, Frodo. You too, Jess," Colton said pulling Brandon into a big side hug by the head and kissing his forehead. "Bring your suds upstairs and check out our pièce de résistance." Colton turned and ran very nimbly up the stairs for a naked, former tight end for the Oregon Ducks.

Jesse and Brandon looked at each other and then over to Ben, who rolled his eyes and motioned for them to head on up the stairs. At the top, the hallway overlooked the big great room and the huge glass wall. The rookies took all of it in with quiet but sincere admiration. They followed Colton's big rounded buns into the bedroom and then around the corner to one of the biggest spa-type bathrooms either had ever seen. There was a large double sink vanity area, a large soaking tub that could hold two men for sure, and in the corner, the largest walk in shower they had ever seen outside of a school or worksite. The shower chamber was glass on the outer walls, slate tiles on the walls. There were two large rain head shower fixtures above and six other shower heads in the walls. There was a television screen and speakers for music or video. It was the shower of the gods.

Brandon summed it up well. "Fuck me," he said in complete awe.

"That's the general idea, Frodo," Colton said, ruffling Brandon's hair. It has amazing pressure, steam sauna, and a great draining system that can handle all the jizz we put down it," Colton said with obvious pride.

Jesse touched the glass doors. "I had no idea firefighting paid this well."

Ben laughed. "We do ok with all the OT, but to be fair, I sort of sold a house of my uncle's that he had left to me and my brother. We used a bunch of that to add the bells and whistles to the house that we wanted. And we have a big mortgage. But it's worth it most of the time."

Colton drained the last of his beer and walked into the shower and pressed some buttons. The overhead rain heads came on and began to spray his large frame. "Don't be shy, boys. Come on in."

Ben walked over to the shower with four big towels and laid them on a bench beside the door. He slid his underwear off and joined Colton under the shower, the two of them wrapped in a big embrace and kissing.

Jesse shrugged and looked at Brandon. Brandon was already stripping off his shirt and pants while trying to hold his beer as well. Jesse took the beer and downed the remains of both the bottles and set them on the vanity. He stripped his work clothes off and followed Brandon's ass into the shower. It was only then he remembered the damn plug up both their holes. He stood under the beautiful shower head with Brandon and reached around to his ass and wiggled the plug. Brandon's eyes widened and it was clear he had forgotten about the butt plug as well.

"You ready to get rid of this thing," Ben said moving over and rubbing his hand against Brandon's wet ass cheeks, pressing on the plug."

"Oh hell yeah," Brandon said. "But shouldn't we like…you know, make sure it's all okay down there?"

"Don't worry about that, little dude. I bet you are pretty cleaned out still," Colton said moving over and sliding his hand down to Jesse's ass. He gripped the plug and pulled it out with a loud pop, letting it drop to the shower floor. Ben dug the black rubber stopper out of Brandon's hole and let it drop as well.

Brandon closed his eyes. His ass felt empty, hollow, and strangely missing something. Ben gripped Brandon and moved him gently over the side of the shower and pressed another button and one of the side shower heads began to pulse and massage his ass cheeks with a soft, hot spray. The way the water danced over the surface of his butt, it took all of 10 seconds for Brandon to begin to chub up. Then Ben reached behind him and gripped the young guy's round butt cheeks and spread the mounds apart and the jet began to pulse inside his weary anus. Brandon moaned and laid his head against Ben's hairy chest and allowed the water to flow inside his tired hole.

"Riding that plug wasn't so bad, was it?" Ben said softly in Brandon's ear.

"No," Brandon answered. He reached forward and wrapped his hand around Ben's thick and swollen member.

"You want my cock inside you, don't you?"

If you enjoyed this sample then look for <u>Shower of Power</u>.

Also by this Author

About the Author

Angus MacGregor resides with his family in Oregon and Hawaii. Along with his passion for writing, Angus enjoys growing orchids, snorkeling and hiking.

Angus has worked as a school teacher, a financial analyst, and a small business developer. He currently works as a writer and supports firefighting efforts by working on wildfires in the US during the summer months. In addition to his adult erotica books, Angus has recently completed his first book of mainstream fiction.

"I love seeing what the Universe has in store for me as I create this reality. I love my life and the blessings of all the people and gifts that surround me. I wish peace and blessings to all my readers."

From the Author

Check my blog for Updates and interesting info.

Author Blog - angus-macgregor.awesomeauthors.org

If you enjoyed any of my books then please share the love and click like on my books in Amazon.

If you write me a review and send me an email I will send you a free book, or many.
(Just know that these emails are filtered by my publisher.)

Good news is always welcome.

One Last Thing, For Kindle Readers...

When you turn the page, Kindle will give you the opportunity to rate this book and share your thoughts on Facebook and Twitter. If you enjoyed my writings, would you please take a few seconds to let your friends know about it? Because... when they enjoy they will be grateful to you and so will I.

Thank You!

Angus MacGregor
angus_macgregor@awesomeauthors.org